Parent's Introduction

Whether your child is a beginning reader, a reluctant reader, or an eager reader, this book offers a fun and easy way to encourage and help your child in reading.

Developed with reading education specialists, **We Both Read** books invite you and your child to take turns reading aloud. You read the left-hand pages of the book, and your child reads the right-hand pages—which have been written at one of six early reading levels. The result is a wonderful new reading experience and faster reading development!

You may find it helpful to read the entire book aloud your-self the first time, then invite your child to participate the second time. As you read, try to make the story come alive by reading with expression. This will help to model good fluency. It will also be helpful to stop at various points to discuss what you are reading. This will help increase your child's understanding of what is being read.

In some books, a few challenging words are introduced in the parent's text, distinguished with **bold** lettering. Pointing out and discussing these words can help to build your child's reading vocabulary. If your child is a beginning reader, it may be helpful to run a finger under the text as each of you reads. Please also notice that a "talking parent" ☺ icon precedes the parent's text, and a "talking child" ☺ icon precedes the child's text.

If your child struggles with a word, you can encourage "sounding it out," but keep in mind that not all words can be sounded out. Your child might pick up clues about a word from the picture, other words in the sentence, or any rhyming patterns. If your child struggles with a word for more than five seconds, it is usually best to simply say the word.

Most of all, remember to praise your child's efforts and keep the reading fun. After you have finished the book, ask a few questions and discuss what you have read together. Rereading this book multiple times may also be helpful for your child.

Try to keep the tips above in mind as you read together, but don't worry about doing everything right. Simply sharing the enjoyment of reading together will increase your child's reading skills and help to start your child off on a lifetime of reading enjoyment!

Dragons Do Not Share!

A We Both Read Book
Level PK–K

Text Copyright © 2018 by D.J. Panec
Illustrations Copyright © 2018 by Andy Elkerton
All rights reserved

We Both Read® is a trademark of Treasure Bay, Inc.

Published by Treasure Bay, Inc.
P.O. Box 119
Novato, CA 94948 USA

Printed in Malaysia

Library of Congress Catalog Card Number: 2017908527

ISBN: 978-1-60115-306-7

Visit us online at:
TreasureBayBooks.com

PR-11-17

WE BOTH READ®

Dragons Do Not Share!

By D.J. Panec

Illustrated by Andy Elkerton

TREASURE BAY

Sam was a dragon who did not want to share.

He did not want to share his crayons. He did
not want to share his . . .

. . . cars.

Many young dragons don't like to share. That's just the way they are.

Sam did not want to share his books or his building toys or his old, torn treasure . . .

. . . map.

One day Sam's cousin, Tess, came to visit. Sam's mother asked him to share his toys with her, but Sam said, . . .

. . . "No."

Sam told his mother, "Dragons never share."

His mother said, "Sam, that isn't true. Don't I share my hugs with **you**? Don't I share my books with **you**? Don't I share my cookies with . . .

. . . **you?**"

Sam's mother held up the sheet of **cookies** she was making and blew a big breath over them, instantly baking the **cookies** to perfection.

Sam's mother gave Sam a small bag of . . .

. . . **cookies.**

 "Would you please take these cookies outside and share them with Tess?" said Sam's mother.

Sam took the bag and went outside with Tess, but Sam did not want to share. He ate a whole cookie with one big **bite**. Then he ate a second cookie with another big . . .

. . . bite.

Sam did not offer Tess a cookie.

Tess didn't say anything, but she looked a little . . .

. . . sad.

Sam told Tess that he had a new **red** scooter.
Tess smiled and said that her favorite color was . . .

. . . **red.**

Sam showed Tess some cool tricks he could do on his scooter. Tess clapped when he flew off the ground and did a perfect loop. Then Tess asked Sam if she could have a turn, but Sam said, . . .

. . . "No."

Sam told Tess that he didn't want to **share**.

He didn't want to **share** his cookies. He didn't want to **share** his scooter. He just didn't want to . . .

. . . share.

Tess looked even sadder now. She turned her back to Sam, but he could tell that she was starting to cry.

Sam began to feel . . .

. . . bad.

"Sorry, Tess," said Sam. "I'm not being mean. I just don't want to share."

"It's OK," Tess replied. "I don't need a turn. I brought a **book** with me, and I think I'd rather read my . . .

. . . book."

Sam did some more tricks on his scooter, but it wasn't as much fun without **Tess**.

Sam took the last cookie from the bag. He was about to eat the cookie with a big bite, but then he thought about . . .

. . . Tess.

Sam thought about how sad Tess looked. Then he remembered a time when he was really sad and how his mother helped him to feel better.

Sam put the cookie back into the . . .

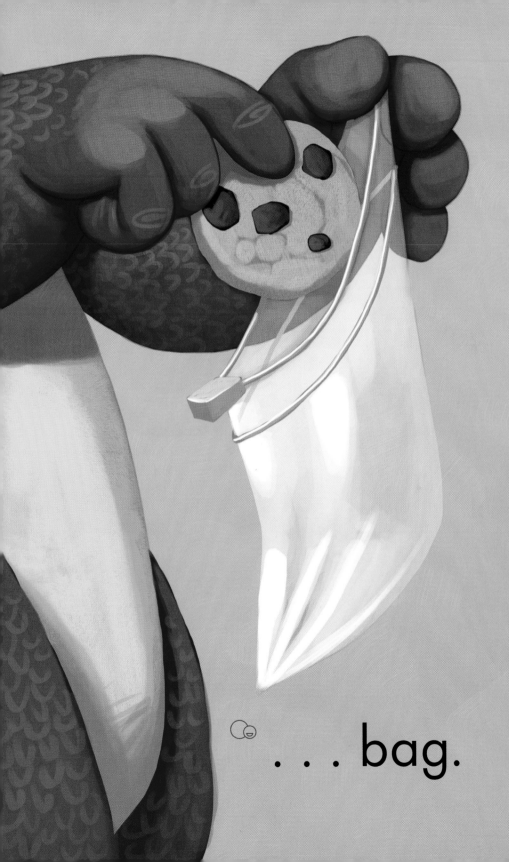

. . . bag.

Sam found Tess reading her book. "There's one more **cookie**," said Sam. "Would you like to have it?"

Tess seemed surprised but said, "Thanks, Sam, I *would* like to have a . . .

. . . **cookie."**

Tess broke the cookie in half. "Here," she said. "We can share it."

Now Sam seemed surprised. "No," he said. "That's nice of **you**, but I already had two cookies. That one is for . . .

. . . you."

Tess smiled and ate the cookie in two big bites.

Then she pointed at the **holes** all over Sam's yard and said, "Why are there so many . . .

. . . holes?"

"I've been digging for treasure," Sam answered.
"I have a treasure map, but it's ripped. I'm missing
the part where the treasure is marked with an . . .

. . . X."

"I have part of a treasure map, too!" exclaimed Tess.

She held her map next to Sam's map. The two maps fit together and showed them exactly where to . . .

38

. . . dig!

Sam and Tess shared the work of digging at the spot marked with an X. And when they found the treasure, they were both very happy to . . .

. . . share.

If you liked **Dragons Do Not Share!,** here are some other
We Both Read® books you are sure to enjoy!

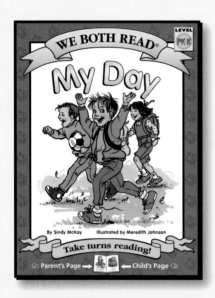

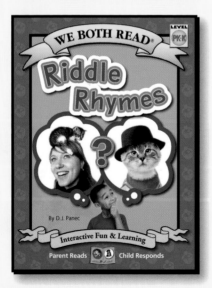

To see all the We Both Read books that are available,
just go online to **www.WeBothRead.com**.